Miguel Tanco
Count on me

Tundra Books, an imprint of Penguin Random House Canada Young Readers,
a Penguin Random House Company

Library and Archives Canada Cataloguing in Publication

Tanco, Miguel, 1972–, author, illustrator
      Count on me / Miguel Tanco.
Issued in print and electronic formats.

ISBN 978-0-7352-6575-2 (hardcover).—ISBN 978-0-7352-6574-5 (EPUB)
    I. Title.
PZ7.1.T375Co 2019   j863'.7   C2018-903156-5
                           C2018-903157-3

Published simultaneously in the United States of America by Tundra Books of Northern New York,
an imprint of Penguin Random House Canada Young Readers, a Penguin Random House Company

Library of Congress Control Number: 2018952543

Edited by Samantha Swenson
Designed by Alice Nussbaum and Five Seventeen
The artwork in this book was rendered in ink and watercolor.
The text was set in 2011 Slimtype and Marianna.
Published by arrangement with Debbie Bibo Agency

Printed and bound in China

www.penguinrandomhouse.ca

1 2 3 4 5   23 22 21 20 19

Penguin
Random House
tundra | TUNDRA BOOKS

Miguel Tanco
Count on me

tundra

At home, everyone
has a passion.
My dad has one.

And my mom
has another one.

My brother loves music,
and he's getting very good at it.

At school, there are all sorts of activities that could be my passion.

I've tried them all,
but they just aren't for me.

There is one thing I really like, though . . .

MATH!

Math is all around us.
It's often hidden,
and I love finding it.

There are geometric shapes on
the playground.

And when we go to the lake, I skip stones to see the concentric circles form in the water.

We live in a world of shapes,
and I like to play with them.

It's fun for me to find
the perfect curve . . .

And solve difficult group problems.

I use math every day.

I know that my passion
can be hard to understand.

But there are infinite ways to see the world . . .

And math is one of them.

FRACTALS

fractal
of three

A fractal is a never-ending pattern.
The patterns used in fractals can be different ~~sizes~~
sizes and directions and are used over and over
to create an ongoing construction. I see lots of
fractals in nature!

BASIC POLYGONS →

A polygon is a flat shape with straight sides that is fully closed. Polygons can have any number of sides. I love to play at finding polygons hidden in objects.

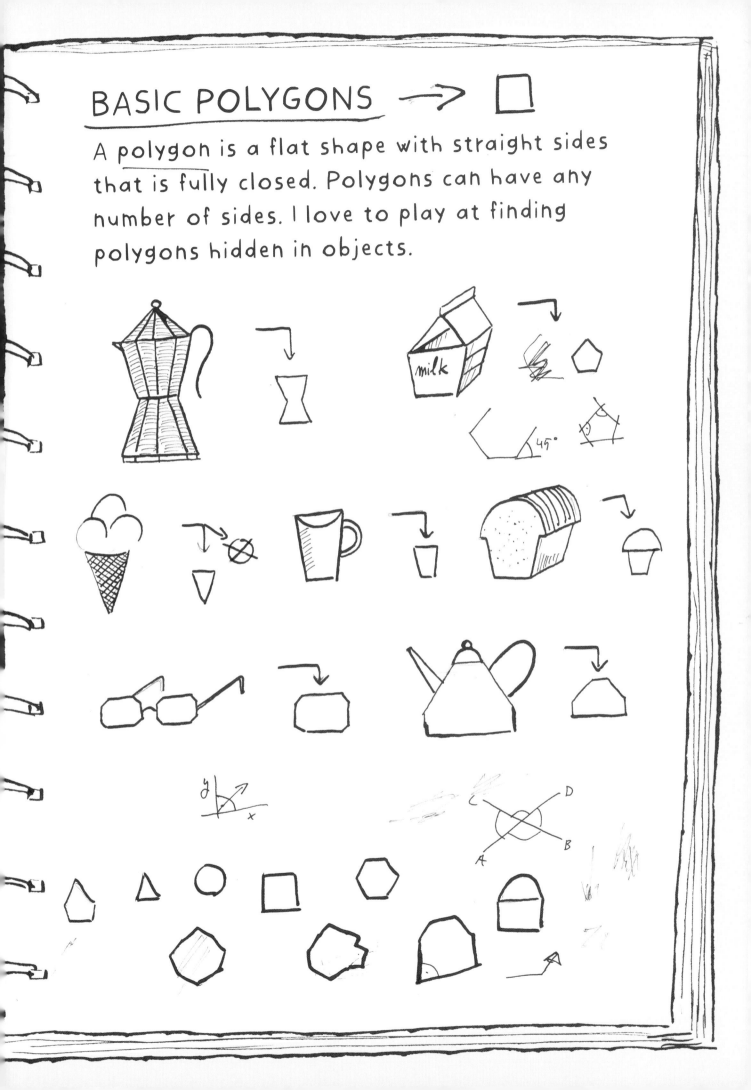

CONCENTRIC CIRCLES

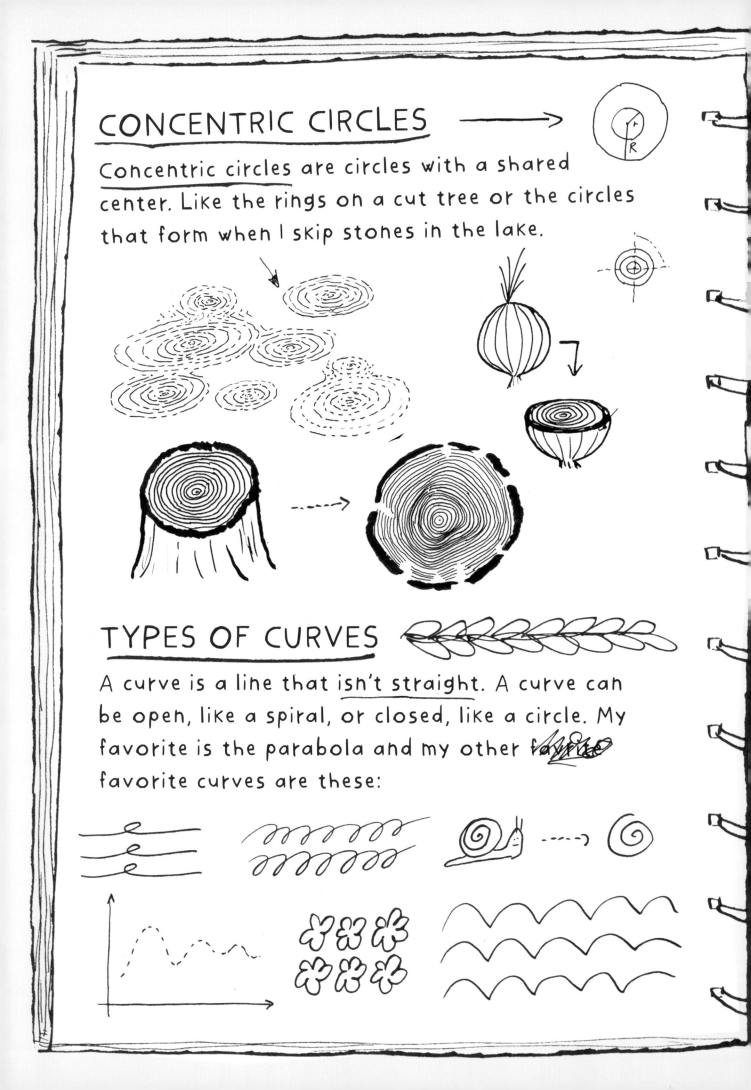

Concentric circles are circles with a shared center. Like the rings on a cut tree or the circles that form when I skip stones in the lake.

TYPES OF CURVES

A curve is a line that isn't straight. A curve can be open, like a spiral, or closed, like a circle. My favorite is the parabola and my other ~~favorite~~ favorite curves are these:

SOLID FIGURES

Solid figures are shapes that are three-dimensional. I know the names of some solid figure shapes:

Sphere

Cylinder

Rectangular Prism

Pyramid

Cube

Cone

TYPES OF TRAJECTORIES

A <u>trajectory</u> is a curved path on which an object moves through space. I see trajectories when a soccer ball is kicked or when someone is on a swing. I like to try to predict the trajectories of my paper airplanes.

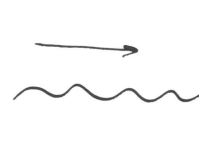

KINDS OF SETS

A set is a group or a collection of things that have at least one common ~~aka~~ characteristic. They can be intersected, added and divided into smaller sets called subsets.

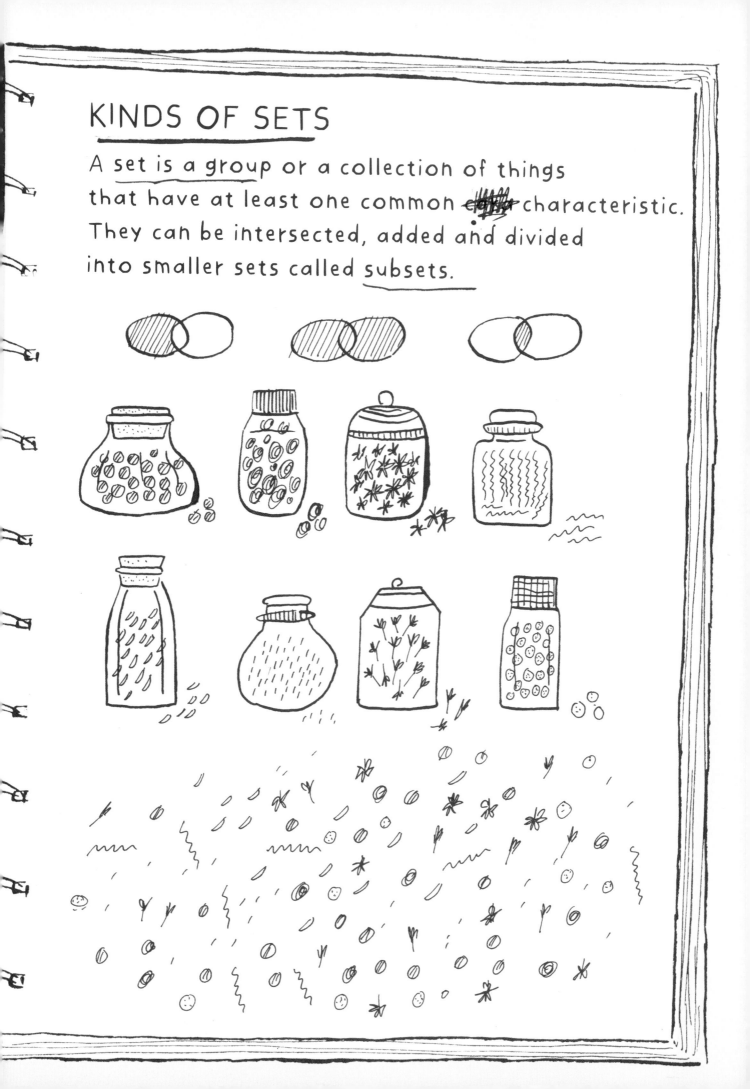

To the people
who follow their passion
and reach the stars

M.T.